In many urban environments, v[...]dered cool. Due to a lac[...] many inner city youth r[...] methods in making a living.

HUNTER STREET

CASHBY STREET

How can you stand up on your feet all day making eight dollars a hour ?

Hard work pays off.

Atlanta, Georgia

Tyrone is Sixteen years old. He recently got hired at a restaurant near his house.
While walking to work, Tyrone is approached by a group of boys, harassing him about his job. The boys try to persuade Tyrone to quit his job.
Tyrone ignores the boys and continues walking to work.

RESTAURANT

After a ten minute walk down Cashby Street,
Tyrone arrives at work.

Tyrone's manager, Mr. Walker opens the door so
Tyrone can enter into the restaurant.

Mr. Walker gives Tyrone different task
to complete as he starts his shift.

Tyrone takes the trash outside; then he mops the floor.

After completing his tasks, Tyrone turns on the grill and fryer. The first customer of the day orders a number one. The number one consists of a double cheeseburger, fries and a drink.

The restaurant was extremely busy for a Monday. Tyrone was unable to take a break . Before closing the restaurant, Tyrone mops the floor and empties the trash. Mr. Walker counts the money from the register and puts it in the safe.

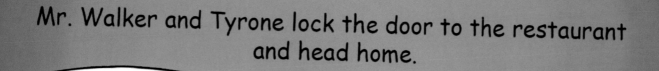

Mr. Walker and Tyrone lock the door to the restaurant and head home.

Tyrone begins his ten minute walk home. While walking home, Tyrone is approached by Mel and Lil Jerry. Mel and Lil Jerry harass Tyrone about his Job. Tyrone ignores Mel and Lil Jerry and continues to walk home.

When Tyrone arrives home, he irons his work clothes for the next day. After ironing his work clothes, Tyrone goes to sleep.

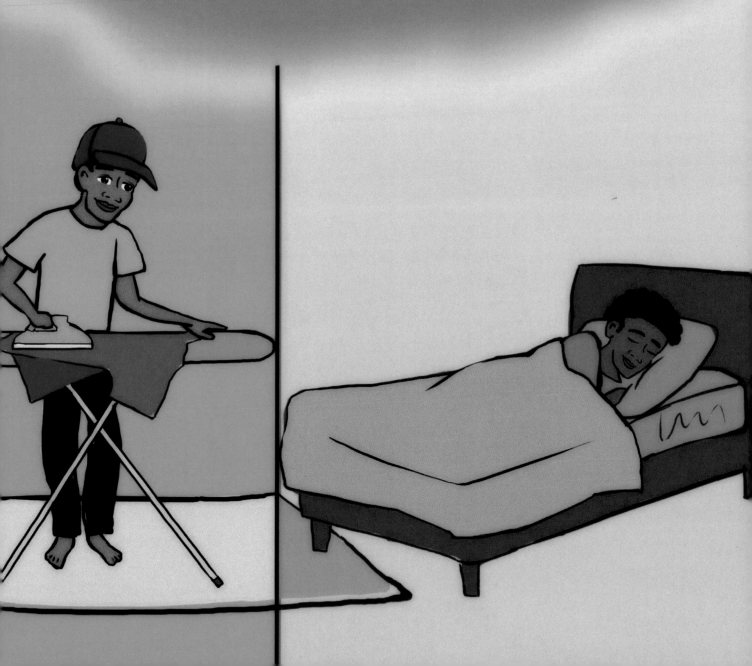

The next morning Tyrone is awakened by his alarm clock.

After eating breakfast Tyrone walks to work. While walking to work, Tyrone sees a police officer arresting Lil Jerry.

Tyrone arrives to work fifteen minutes early.
Mr. Walker compliments Tyrone for his hard work
and his dedication to the job.

The restaurant was extremely busy from lunchtime to closing.

Before the shift ended, Mr. Walker passes out paychecks to all employees.

The next morning Tyrone wakes up early to deposit
his check into his bank account.
Tyrone saves seventy percent of his money and lives off
the remaining thirty percent.

After leaving the bank, Tyrone heads to work.
While walking to work Tyrone passes Mel and Lil Jerry.
Lil Jerry was released from jail earlier that morning.
Mel and Lil Jerry
harass Tyrone as usual about working a job.

Tyrone arrives at work fifteen minutes early. Mr. Walker opens the door for Tyrone and tells him he needs to talk to him. Tyrone and Mr. Walker walk to the back office. Mr. Walker offers Tyrone a position as supervisor and gives him a two dollar raise. Tyrone accepts the position as supervisor.

The food truck returns later that day, before the restaurant closes, to deliver the missing boxes of fries.

Tyrone begins his ten minute walk home. While walking home, Tyrone is approached by Mel and Lil Jerry. Mel and Lil Jerry harass Tyrone about his Job. Tyrone ignores Mel and Lil Jerry and continues to walk home.

After a fifteen minute walk from work,
Tyrone arrives home. Tyrone turns on his stereo
and falls asleep.

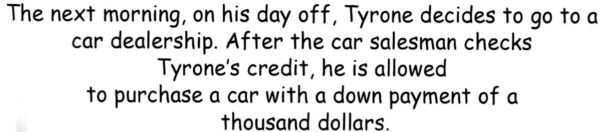

The next morning, on his day off, Tyrone decides to go to a car dealership. After the car salesman checks Tyrone's credit, he is allowed to purchase a car with a down payment of a thousand dollars.

After purchasing his car,
Tyrone drives home. Tyrone passes Mel and Lil Jerry
on his way home.

Tyrone parks his car in the driveway and walks in the house.
Tyrone's mother is looking out of the window when he drives up.

After talking to his mother Tyrone goes to his room.

Tyrone I'm so proud of you.

Tyrone irons his clothes before he goes to bed.
Around ten o'clock p.m. Tyrone falls asleep.

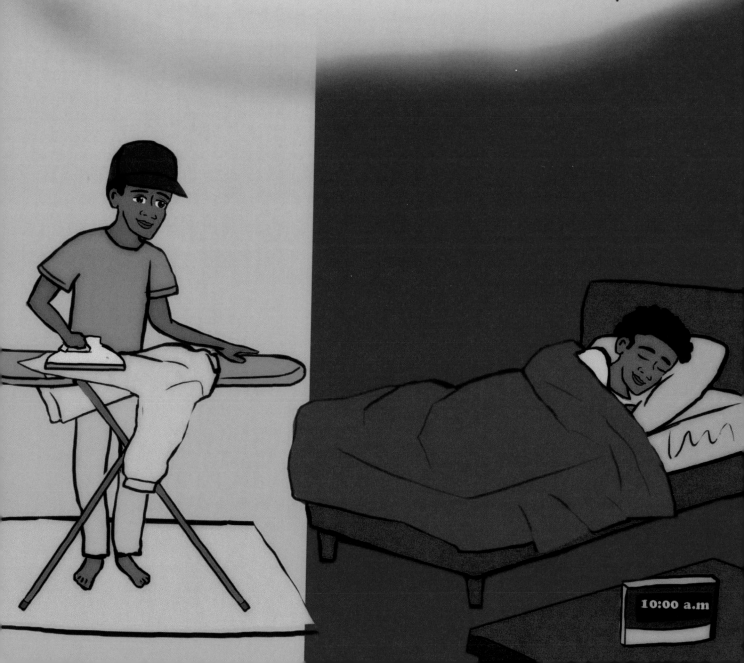

Tyrone's alarm clock wakes him up at six o' clock in the morning. Tyrone gets up, brushes his teeth and takes a shower.

After eating breakfast
Tyrone starts his car and pulls out of the driveway.

While driving to work Tyrone see's Mel and Lil Jerry getting arrested on the corner of Cashby and Hunter Street.

The employees prepare for the lunch rush.

Mel and Lil Jerry come to the restaurant to order some food. While ordering food, they harass Tyrone about his job.

Mel and Lil Jerry flash a large amount of money in the restaurant.

After the lunch rush, the restaurant was extremely slow, so Tyrone closes the restaurant early.

While driving home from work, Tyrone sees
Mel and Lil Jerry getting arrested again.

Ten minutes later, Tyrone arrives home. Tyrone parks
his car in the driveway and walks in the house.
Tyrone watches television for an hour before going to bed.

When Tyrone starts school he will only be
able to work four days a week.

The next morning Tyrone eats breakfast before he goes to work.

After eating breakfast Tyrone starts his car and heads to work.

While driving to work Tyrone doesn't see Mel and Lil Jerry on Cashby and Hunter Street because they are still in jail.

Tyrone continues to work at the restaurant until he graduates from high school. After graduating from high school he enrolls in college. Tyrone decides to major in sociology.

Mel and Lil Jerry continue to get arrested at the corner of Casby and Hunter Street. After multiple arrests Mel and Lil Jerry have to serve time in prison.

Hook: Slow money Slow money better than no money

If you get caught on the block do you got bail money

What if you get caught making a sell homie

Slow money Slow money better than no money

Slow money Slow money better than no money

Verse:

Ain't nothing wrong with working a nine to five and Punching the Clock

Let them call you lame Lil homie get right

When you buy that new car they will see it right

Even If they don't you on a path my brother

Paradise never think gutter

Program to think a certain way it ain't our fault

Even though it's a system I'm addressing these issues

Refusing to stay in the same spot cause life is bout progression

Even having a Lil motion believe that's a blessing

In everything you do you got to have a plan

Hear what I said you got to have a plan

Ain't nothing cool bout being locked in a can

Life is what you make of it yes you can

Believe me you can be anything you wannabe man

Just be yourself and not a wannabe man

Individuality goes a long way fam

Some folk Some Folks ain't gone understand

Glossary

Paycheck – Money for labor paid to employees.

Deposit – to put money in a bank account.

Supervisor- a person in charge of day to day operations of employees in a business.

Inventory- a stock of items.

Credit- to borrow money.

Harass- to insult constantly.

Sociology- the systematic study of human society and social interactions.

Thank you for taking the opportunity to purchase and read my book I really appreciate it.

www.rashadpatterson.com

RASHAD PATTERSON

Made in the USA
Monee, IL
20 May 2021